ROBIN HOOD AND

This Walker Double contains two great stories about Robin Hood and his arch enemy, the Sheriff of Nottingham.

Julian Atterton aims to write the kind of stories that he enjoyed reading when he was a child. "I used to long for strange adventures with wonderful companions," he says. Twice shortlisted for the Young Observer Fiction Prize, he is the author of several exciting historical stories – *The Last Harper*, *The Fire of the Kings*, *The Tournament of Fortune*, *Knights of the Sacred Blade*, *Knights of the Lost Domain*, *The Shape-Changer* and another Sherwood Forest tale, *The Outlaw, Robin Hood* (1996). When he is not writing and researching, he likes to indulge in his favourite hobby, rock-climbing. He lives on the north Yorkshire moors.

Robin Hood
—— and the ——
Sheriff

JULIAN ATTERTON

Illustrations by
GARETH FLOYD

WALKER BOOKS
AND SUBSIDIARIES
LONDON • BOSTON • SYDNEY

First published 1995 by Walker Books Ltd
87 Vauxhall Walk, London SE11 5HJ

4 6 8 10 9 7 5 3

This book has been typeset in Plantin.

Printed in England by Clays Ltd, St Ives plc

British Library Cataloguing in Publication Data
A catalogue record for this book is
available from the British Library.

ISBN 0-7445-2490-3

CONTENTS

Robin Hood and the Sheriff

1. The Knight...9

2. The Abbot's Charity 21

3. A Craftsman and His Wares 31

4. The White Hart of Sherwood 41

The Golden Arrow

1. A Quarrel at Daybreak 53

2. Roast Goose and Archery.................62

3. Guests of the Sheriff........................74

4. Robin and Marian............................88

Robin Hood
and
The Sheriff

1. The Knight

A lone traveller was riding through the Forest of Barnsdale. He was lost in thought, trusting his horse to follow the road, and he did not see the three outlaws who stood among the trees ahead, watching him approach.

"He wears a sword, so he must be a knight," said the smallest of the three, whose name was Much.

"There's nothing fancy about his clothes," said the tallest, whose name was Little John. "He may be a knight, but he does not look rich."

"He may be rich but trying hard not to look it," said the eldest, Will Scarlet. "Either way, he looks to me the kind Robin sent us here to welcome."

For they were outlaws with Robin Hood, and there by the road on his orders.

The traveller dismounted to let his horse drink from a trough at the wayside. He stooped to wash his face, and when he looked up he found himself ringed by three men dressed in foresters' clothes of Lincoln green.

"Welcome to Barnsdale," said Little John. "Might we ask your name and where you are bound?"

The traveller squared his shoulders and faced the outlaws with a stare. "My name is Sir Richard of Lee," he replied, "but

where I ride is none of your business."

"We only ask because we hope you'll not mind breaking your journey," said Will Scarlet. "Our master sent us here to find a guest to dine with him."

As Will was speaking, Little John took hold of the knight's horse by the bridle, and Sir Richard saw that this was an invitation he had very little choice but to accept.

The outlaws led him deep into the forest by narrow tracks that wound through the thickets and shadows until they caught the smell of woodsmoke and roasting meat and followed it to a glade by a stream. Gathered there, round a cooking-fire, were a band of men dressed in the colours of the greenwood, their leader a young man with a red beard who sprang to his feet with a shout of greeting when Sir Richard and his guides came into sight.

"Here's our guest, Robin," Little John called out to him. "He calls himself Sir Richard of Lee."

"You are welcome, Sir Richard," said Robin, "and you are just in time to do us the honour of carving the meat."

So it was that Sir Richard of Lee found himself sitting among outlaws, eating the King's venison. He was surprised by his own appetite. When he had eaten his fill of roast he was offered bean-bread and cheese, and as he washed the crumbs down with a sup of ale, he turned to Robin with a smile.

"That was the heartiest meal I have eaten for many weeks," he said. "I thank you."

"We make it a custom of the forest that our guests pay for their dinner," said Robin. "What gift will you make us, Sir Richard?"

The knight untied the wallet at his belt and offered it to his host. "You are welcome to my money," he said. "I wish there were more."

The wallet held only a few silver pennies. Robin glanced at Little John, who had gone through the knight's saddle-bags while their owner was eating, and Little John nodded. "How far are you riding?" Robin asked the knight.

"To York," replied Sir Richard, and his face looked suddenly careworn. "I must leave you now and be on my way," he said.

"We'll not take your money," said Robin, "but tell us why a gallant man like yourself is riding to a fine city like York with so heavy a heart."

Sir Richard shook his head. "I'll not spoil the taste of a good meal with the tale of my troubles."

"All of us around this fire have troubles," said Robin.

Sir Richard looked around their faces. "What you see in me, my friends," he said, "is a man who has been unlucky enough to make an enemy of the Sheriff of Nottingham."

"We have heard of him," said Robin, and the outlaws laughed.

"Then you will know how he lets his men run wild and take whatever they want," said Sir Richard. "They attacked my son, and when he killed one of them in his own defence, he was dragged to Nottingham and the Sheriff sent to tell me that unless I could pay four hundred pounds to buy his pardon, my son would be hung as a murderer. What could I do? All I have is my land, and my land is my son's inheritance. I went to Nottingham and begged for mercy. The Sheriff has hated me for years, and he laughed in my face, but one of the guests at his table took pity and lent me the four hundred pounds in return for my pledge that my land would be his if I could not pay him back in a year and a day. So my son was saved, but the Sheriff has harried me from that day to this, and folk live in such fear of him that I have been unable to borrow a single penny."

"What is the name of the man who lent you the money?" asked Robin.

"He is the Abbot of Saint Mary's in York," replied Sir Richard. "I am on my way to beg him for more time."

"And if he refuses, you will lose your land?" asked Robin.

"And the Sheriff will have won," Sir Richard said bitterly.

Robin turned to Much the Miller's son.
"Go to the hiding-place," he told him.
"Count four hundred pounds from the
hoard and pack them into saddle-bags."
Sir Richard gasped. Robin turned to Will
Scarlet and Little John. "If we are going
to lend Sir Richard our treasure," he said,
"some of us had better ride with him to
protect him from being robbed."

2. The Abbot's Charity

The Abbot of Saint Mary's was at table with his old friend and guest, the Sheriff of Nottingham.

"Are you certain that Sir Richard will come empty-handed?" he asked the Sheriff.

"He has not been able to raise the money in Nottinghamshire," replied the Sheriff, grinning through his black beard. "I have seen to that."

"Then his land will be mine, and I will sell it to you as we agreed," the Abbot said contentedly.

Listening to them was the Prior, who could hardly believe his ears. "You cannot rob a man of his land," he protested.

"Stay out of matters you do not understand," the Abbot warned him, and it was at that very moment that the porter came in to announce that Sir Richard had arrived. The Abbot and Sheriff sat back, rubbing their hands, but when Sir Richard came in they saw that he was not alone. With him were two men in Lincoln green, one so small that he barely reached Sir Richard's shoulder and the other so tall that his head almost grazed the rafters of the Abbot's hall.

Sir Richard stared angrily at the Sheriff. "I should have known I would find you here, my lord," he told him. "I

suppose you have come to gloat."

"I am here only to see that justice is
done," the Sheriff replied smugly, but he
was unsettled enough by the look of Sir
Richard's companions to whisper to the
squire who stood at his shoulder, who at
once hurried out of the hall.

Sir Richard faced the Abbot with
bowed head. "I must confess that I left

home without the money I owe you," he said. "I have come to throw myself upon your charity and beg you to grant me the grace of another year before you hold me to my pledge."

The Abbot shifted uncomfortably in his chair, for Sir Richard's words had touched him, but he held to his purpose and made his face a mask of sternness and sorrow. "I wish it were within my power to grant what you ask," he said, "but I have many burdens and responsibilities, and I must have either my four hundred pounds or the land you pledged if you could not repay."

Sir Richard turned to Much and Little John – who were his two companions – and gave a sigh. "It seems I must gratefully accept your help," he said.

Little John swung a bulging saddle-bag
onto the table in front of the Abbot,
where it landed with a thump that made
the wine-cups jump.

"There are your four hundred pounds,
my lord," Sir Richard told the Abbot. "I
thank you for the loan of them and ask
you to declare before these witnesses that
any claim you have to my land ends here

and now with their repayment."

The Abbot's mouth fell open, giving him the look of a fish on a market-stall, but the Sheriff sat forward with clenched fists. "Who are these men?" he asked Sir Richard.

"That is no affair of yours, my lord," Sir Richard told him. "You have the four hundred pounds I paid for my son's pardon, and my lord Abbot has the money I borrowed from him to pay you. I am free of you both."

The Sheriff rose to his feet. "I will ask you once more, Sir Richard," he said. "Who are these men and how did they come by this money? How are we to know this money is not stolen?"

"This might be a wise moment for you to leave," Sir Richard whispered to Much and Little John, and as he was speaking, the Sheriff's men-at-arms marched into the hall and lined up, barring the way to the door.

"Only six?" asked Little John. "We'll soon make them wish they'd stayed in bed." He took hold of the bench that ran the length of the Abbot's table, lifted it to the height of his shoulders and flung it in the faces of the men-at-arms with a force that knocked three to the floor and made the others jump sideways to save themselves. Much and Little John leapt

over the bench and the flailing legs and
arms of those pinned beneath and ran out
through the door into the monks' court.

"Catch them," roared the Sheriff,
but by the time his men had picked themselves up and set off in pursuit, Much
and Little John were safely through the

abbey gate and had vanished into the maze of alleyways that ran between the houses of the city of York.

The Sheriff's gaze went from the saddle-bag to Sir Richard. "So you refuse to tell me where this money is from?" he asked.

Sir Richard smiled but made no reply.

"Then I accuse you of robbery," the Sheriff said darkly. "I intend to learn the truth of this, and you will rot in chains until I do."

3. A Craftsman and His Wares

His elbows on the ledge of a loft-window beneath a high thatched gable, Robin Hood looked down on the bustling street. When at last he saw the face he was waiting for, he turned inside to Much and Little John.

"Will is back," he said, and they waited impatiently until the ladder creaked and Will Scarlet clambered up to join them.

"The Sheriff has taken Sir Richard back to his lodging," Will said breathlessly. "It lies over the river, on Bishopshill, a fine hall with a gated yard.

The Sheriff has his wife and half his household with him."

"I say we wait till they are asleep, then climb over the gate," said Little John.

Will shook his head. "One mistake and the whole neighbourhood will be awake," he said. "What do you say, Robin?"

Robin had returned to the window and was gazing at the wares in the doorway of a potter's shop on the other side of the street. "How much money do we have with us?" he asked.

"I brought the red purse from the hiding-place," said Much.

"Well done," said Robin. "That should be enough to buy all we need."

At the hour of vespers, when the smell of cooking wafted out to join the rich smells of the street, a man in a potter's

apron rode over the Ousebridge on a
covered cart drawn by a mule. He trotted
slowly up Bishopshill and drew rein at
the arched gateway of a tall house in the
shadow of the city wall.

"My name is Lucas the Potter," he told
the man-at-arms who stood in the gate.
"Ask your good lady of Nottingham if
she would care to see my wares."

Now it just so happened that the

Sheriff and his wife – the lady Clara – were in the middle of a boiling quarrel, and it was the Sheriff who was getting scalded. When the man-at-arms appeared at the door of their chamber, the Sheriff listened to his message and nodded eagerly.

"Send him up," he ordered, and he turned to his wife. "Buy whatever you want, my love. Nothing is too good for my little rosebud."

"Do not think for a minute that you can weasel your way around me with a few pots," the lady Clara hissed at him, but she did not hiss quite as loudly as she had been hissing a moment before.

Into their chamber stepped a man with a red beard and a large potter's apron tied around his waist.

"Greetings, my lord and lady," said Robin Hood as two of the Sheriff's men came panting up the stairs carrying baskets which they set down with great relief. As they left, Robin closed the door of the chamber. From its nest of sacking and straw he pulled an earthenware jug with patterns around the rim and a bright green glaze. The lady Clara gave a murmur of admiration, but from the room below came the sound of a shout followed by a crash.

"What the devil are they up to down in the kitchen?" asked the Sheriff.

"By the sound of it, one of your servants has dropped a pan on his foot," Robin said gaily. "May I beg you to feast your eyes on the glaze of these goblets?"

"How exquisite," said the lady Clara,

and she gripped her husband's sleeve. "Think how they would mirror the shine of our silver plate."

"They would indeed," agreed the Sheriff, whose collection of silver plate was his pride and joy and went with him everywhere. He took a goblet and was admiring the curve of it when from below came the sound of a howl followed by a second and louder crash. The Sheriff looked up to see the Potter drawing a long dagger from the belt beneath his apron, and before the Sheriff could say a word, Robin's arm was outstretched and the tip of the blade was tickling the Sheriff's throat.

"Do not move, my lord Sheriff," said Robin. "Nor you, my lady, unless you want me to present you with your

husband's head in a pot."

"What do you want?" asked the
Sheriff.

"Justice, my lord," replied Robin. "You
are holding Sir Richard of Lee, who has
done you no harm or wrong. I am here to
set him free, and if you are wise, you will
let us leave in peace."

From below came the sound of the cart

clattering out through the gateway into the street. Robin sprang to the door and snatched the key from the lock.

"Do not show your face at the window unless you want your eyebrows joined in the middle by an arrow," he warned the Sheriff, then he stepped outside, locking the Sheriff and his lady fast in their own chamber.

By the time the Sheriff had found the courage to throw open the window-shutters and bellow for help, and by the time he had found his servants and men-at-arms – who were locked in the very cellar where Sir Richard had been locked until his rescuers came – it was dusk, and the Sheriff arrived at the city gate nearest to his lodging to find that it had just been closed and barred for the night. The guards said they well remembered a potter who had ridden out on a covered cart just before nightfall, a man with a red beard who had given them a cheery wave.

The Sheriff stormed back to his lodging to be met by one of his servants, who approached him with a face as pale as cheese. "Your silver plate, my lord," he whispered. "It seems to have vanished."

4. The White Hart of Sherwood

Despite his misfortunes, the Sheriff left York with a smile on his grim face. He had promised himself that when he got home, he would burn Sir Richard's land until it was no more than a smoking waste.

The lady Clara was a fine rider, and they travelled fast. They were on the last day of their journey, and pausing to water their horses at Saint Anne's Well in the southern bounds of Sherwood, when a peasant boy came running up to them.

"Have you come to hunt the white hart, my lord?" he asked the Sheriff.

Never in all his years as a huntsman
had the Sheriff even seen the tracks of
such a creature, so when the boy told of a
white hart with horns as blue as ice which
had been seen that morning on a neigh-
bouring hill, the Sheriff wanted nothing
more than to be after it while the trail was
fresh. He called three of his men to his
side and told his wife and the rest of the

cavalcade to ride on to Nottingham, then he gave the boy a mule and ordered him to lead him to the hart.

When they reached a valley where the forest grew tall, the boy warned them to ride softly, for they were near where the hart had been seen. They were trotting along, straining their ears and scouring the undergrowth with their gaze, when a

man with a red beard leapt down from the trees ahead to block their path.

"Welcome to Sherwood, my lord Sheriff," he called out in greeting.

"I'll give you a welcome, you thief," snarled the Sheriff. His men raised their bows, and it was the last act of their lives. Arrows hissed down from the trees and the men fell gasping as their horses bolted in panic, leaving the Sheriff alone among the outlaws who on every side were swinging down from the branches.

"What in the devil's name more do you want from me?" he asked as they pulled him from his horse.

"Only that you be our guest for dinner," replied Robin.

He led the Sheriff through the trees

towards a smell of woodsmoke and roasting meat which they followed to a clearing where a boar was sizzling over a hearth. When the meat was carved, the Sheriff was galled to see it handed out on his own silver plate, but he managed to overcome his feelings and eat with his usual greed.

Robin waited until his guest had eaten his fill and wiped his lips. "Now, my lord," he said, "what gift will you make the poor folk of Sherwood in return for your meal?"

"I have nothing but the pennies in my purse," replied the Sheriff, patting the wallet on his belt.

Robin glanced at Little John, who emptied the Sheriff's saddle-bag. Out fell four leather purses filled with coins.

Robin weighed them in his hands and fixed the Sheriff with a stare.

"Would these by any chance be the four hundred pounds you made Sir Richard pay you to save his son?" he asked.

The Sheriff stared back and said nothing.

"I say that this money does not belong to you at all, my lord," said Robin. "It belongs to Sir Richard, whose son was falsely accused. We will see that it is safely returned to him, and *you*, my lord Sheriff, will swear now on your soul that you will never seek to harm Sir Richard nor any of his kin."

The Sheriff gave a growl of rage and would have flung himself at Robin's throat had Little John's hands not come down on his shoulders, holding him in his place.

"Swear it," said Robin, "and you will ride home with your silver plate in your saddle-bag as a gift to remind you always of our meeting. Refuse, and it may be your head that bounces into Nottingham in the bag tied to your saddle."

"I swear I will never again seek to harm Sir Richard or his kin," said the Sheriff, staring hatred at Robin with every word.

The outlaws escorted their guest back to the road, led out his horse, and Robin held the Sheriff's stirrup for him to mount. As he settled himself in his saddle, the Sheriff gazed down at the outlaw. "For an oath to be binding," he said, "I have to know the name of the man to whom it is sworn."

"My name is Robin Hood," said
Robin, and he clapped the Sheriff's horse
on the rump to send it galloping on its
way. The Sheriff rode grimly, and late
that night by the glowing hearth in the
great hall of his castle he swore a second
oath all to himself. He swore that before a
year and a day had gone by he would
bring Robin Hood to his doom.

THE
GOLDEN ARROW

1. A Quarrel at Daybreak

As the sun rose over the greenwood, a
herd of deer came to the pool by the packhorse bridge to drink. The forest was so
still that they did not even sense the
delighted gaze of a sleepy man in a large
grey woollen cassock, who lay watching
them from the hollow in the riverbank
where he had just spent the night.

At the sound of hoofbeats, the deer
turned and darted for cover. The Friar
reached for a fallen branch and pulled it
over his hollow so that he was hidden but
could see all he wanted by peering out
between the leaves.

What he saw made him hold his breath in wonder. A maiden in a long green cloak rode up to the far end of the packhorse bridge and dismounted, tethering her palfrey by the pool. She stood gazing up at the forest trees, smiling at the richness of their colours as they turned towards the red and gold of autumn; then she caught the sound of hoofbeats drawing near on the Friar's side of the river, and ran up onto the bridge to meet the approaching rider.

Here the Friar lost sight of her, though he discovered that by wriggling sideways he could see her reflection on the surface of the pool – and running towards her the reflection of a young man with a red beard, who clasped the maiden in his arms in a long and laughing embrace.

The Friar decided that it would be a
fine joke to wait a moment and then pop
up to wish them a cheery good morning,
but as he was biding his time he caught
the sound of their voices, and they were
voices raised in anger.

"Go there and you will be tempting the devil," the maiden said in warning. "The Sheriff has only to set eyes on you and you will hang."

The young man with the red beard shook his head. "Nottingham Fair draws folk from miles around," he said. "We will be ghosts in the crowd."

"Then if it is safe, take me with you," the maiden challenged him.

"If you were with us, everyone with eyes would stare," the young man replied with a laugh.

The maiden pulled away from him. "Go where you will," she said angrily. "All I know is that I cannot bear the worrying that goes with the waiting. I am tired of waiting for you, Robin."

Shaking her head, she turned and

walked towards her horse. The man named Robin stood as if his feet had been nailed to the ground and his tongue tied to his teeth. Only when the maiden had swung up into her saddle and heeled her horse for home did he find his voice.

"Marian," he called out imploringly, but she did not turn back.

Marian Fitzwalter rode blindly, but her tears were all wept and her face dry and pale by the time she rode into the yard of her father's house to find six horses being fed and a squire and four men-at-arms who were passing round a jug of ale. Sitting with her father by his hearth Marian found a pale-eyed knight she had not seen in a long while but recognized all too well, Sir Guy of Gisburn. He sprang to his feet and bowed to her in greeting.

"You are welcome, Sir Guy," she said courteously. "To what do we owe the pleasure of your visit?"

"I am bound for Nottingham Fair and could not ride by without paying my respects," replied Sir Guy. "Have you ever been to the Fair, my lady?"

"No, and I should love to," said Marian.

Sir Guy let his eyes feast on her beauty. "One day you must let me escort you there," he said with a smile.

"I would be happy to ride with you today," declared Marian.

This was more than Sir Guy had hoped, and a good deal more than Marian's father, who thought he knew his daughter's heart better than anyone in the world, could bring himself to believe. "You wish to ride to Nottingham with Sir Guy?" he asked incredulously.

"You need have no fears for your daughter's safety," Sir Guy assured him, spurred by the vision of how glorious he would look at the Fair with Marian at his side. "We will be guests of the Sheriff,

and the lady Marian will be lodged with
every comfort in the women's chamber of
the castle. I promise to escort her
faithfully and to obey her every
command."

It was not Sir Guy's words that
persuaded Sir Gilbert Fitzwalter, but the
look his daughter gave him, imploring
him to agree. "Go then with my
blessing," he said, "and come safely
home."

2. Roast Goose and Archery

Never in her life had Marian been anywhere so crowded. The wide open ground between the old town on Saint Mary's Hill and the newer houses clustered beneath the castle was covered with the booths of merchants come from far and wide, their tented alleyways bustling with customers, jugglers and pastry-sellers.

Marian wandered a whole morning with Sir Guy's squire at her side. She bought silks and spices, but not even the songs of the minstrels could stop her

wondering what she would say if she and Robin came face to face, and when she was not wondering that, she was wondering why she had nowhere caught even a glimpse of him.

Sir Guy came looking for her at midday, having used the morning to get himself shaved and scented and to buy a new surcoat. He sent the squire back to their lodgings in the castle with the silk and spices and swept Marian to a table at one of the cookshops selling roast goose and wine. As they were eating they heard a braying of trumpets on the field below the castle.

"That will be the start of the entertainment," Sir Guy told her, "an archery contest open to all comers. The Sheriff is offering a golden arrow as prize for the winner."

Marian felt the food lose its taste in her mouth. She understood now why Robin had wanted to come: to test his skill with the bow and win the golden arrow. Marian had no doubt that if he were there, Robin would win. He was the finest archer she had ever seen.

"Would it please you to watch the contest?" Sir Guy asked her.

Marian knew that no power on earth could keep her from the archery field, but in the same moment it dawned on her how unbearable it would be for Robin if he caught sight of her with his old enemy Sir Guy of Gisburn at her side. The thought of it was enough to make Marian wish she were curled up in a bucket at the bottom of the deepest well in Nottingham.

"I would be happy to watch if there were a place I could sit quietly in the shade," she answered Sir Guy.

He escorted her to where the ladies of the castle were gathered on cushioned stools in the shadow of an awning, then he himself went to watch with the Sheriff and his knights. Out on the field, the contest was well under way. Arrows were thudding into targets set at a range of sixty paces from the bow.

Some forty archers had come forward
to try their luck. Most wore caps or had
pulled their hoods forward to shield their
eyes from the sun, but no hood could
hide Robin's red beard, and Marian
recognized him by the way he stood
leaning on his bow to watch the others.
When his turn came, she was astonished
by the ease with which he sent his arrow
straight to the centre of its target. Many
of the archers were already at the limit of

their skill, and Robin's marksmanship was drawing gasps and applause.

By his side Marian recognized Will Scarlet, but when the targets were at a hundred paces, Will's arrow fell short and he left the field. When the targets were moved to a hundred and twenty paces, only two of the archers left in the contest were able to get their arrows to strike home, but they both – and one of them was Robin – struck their targets straight in the eye.

Amid rising excitement, a single target was placed at a hundred and forty paces. Robin shot first and sent his arrow straight into the centre of it. His fellow-archer laughed and shook his head, but then took careful aim and struck the eye with his arrow so close to Robin's

that the shafts hummed together and the watching crowd let out a roar of acclaim.

The marshal of the contest called the two archers to speak with him, then the targets were taken away and a peeled hazel wand set upright in the ground at a hundred and fifty paces from the shooting line. The trumpets blared and a herald spoke.

"If it please my lord Sheriff, Adam of Newark and Reynard Greenleaf will now contest the golden arrow. The first to strike the wand shall be the winner."

The Sheriff gave a nod of assent and Adam of Newark was offered first aim. His arrow soared high and fell with a swoop, but it whistled past the wand a clear hand's breadth to one side. Robin stepped forward and notched an arrow to his bow. When he loosed, his arrow flew swift and low, hitting the wand with a crack and splitting it down the middle.

Marian felt as if her heart were about to burst with pride. Trumpets brayed and the Sheriff nodded to one of his squires, who held up a golden arrow which caught the light, glinting in the sunshine.

"Reynard Greenleaf," called the Sheriff. "Come and claim your well-earned reward."

Robin walked towards him as if with great respect, his eyes on the ground and his hood hiding most of his face. When he was within three paces of the Sheriff he froze in his tracks. Men-at-arms were pouring out from behind the awning. Robin turned to run, but too late. He was pulled to the ground and dragged on his

knees to the Sheriff, who threw back his prisoner's hood and stood gazing down at the face of the man he had vowed to destroy.

"Welcome to Nottingham, Robin Hood," the Sheriff said triumphantly.

Marian watched in silent horror as Robin was dragged away to the castle. She did not see the burly friar in a grey cassock who stood watching among the crowd on the far side of the field with a face as stricken as her own, but she could not help but see Sir Guy when he loomed up in front of her, grinning like a wolf.

"Thanks to the Sheriff's cunning, the entertainment is far from over," he said. "Tomorrow morning you will see an outlaw hang."

3. Guests of the Sheriff

Supper with the Sheriff and his
household in the great hall of the castle
was the longest nightmare Marian had
ever lived. When at last the meal was over
and the ladies rose to withdraw, Marian
was grateful to flee, but she did not stay
long with the ladies in their chamber. She
lit a candle and slipped away to the one
place in all the castle where she felt sure
she could be alone in peace – the chapel.

Placing her candle on the altar, she
knelt and prayed. "Sweet Mary, Mother
of Christ, save my love."

She at once heard footsteps, and a man knelt at her side, crossing himself before the altar. Glancing round, Marian saw a friar with kind eyes gazing at her sadly. "Are you praying for Robin Hood?" he asked her.

Marian gasped. "How do you know?"

"That is a tale I cannot bear to tell until Robin is saved," replied the Friar. "I have found a way to save him, but it must be tried at once, before the Sheriff and his men rise from table, and I cannot do it on my own. Will you help?"

The jailer on guard in the keep-tower was idling over the last of his supper when into his chamber walked a pale maiden escorted by a friar as fat as a pumpkin, who held out a purse clinking with silver pennies.

"We beg a moment with Robin Hood," he said. "This fair lady is his sister come to say farewell. I myself have come to hear his confession."

The jailer held out his hand and grinned, and when he had stowed the purse in the wallet on his belt he rose and lit a torch at his brazier and led them down to dark vaults hewn deep into the red rock on which the castle stood. He unlocked a door with a key from the ring on his belt, drew back two bolts and pushed it open. In the dark hole beyond,

a man lay on the ground, his ankles shackled by chains to the wall.

Marian ran to Robin, and as she knelt to take his head in her hands and cover it with kisses, she whispered a torrent of words into his ear. Robin seemed to slump in her arms, and Marian looked around as if in fright.

"He is half-dead," she told the jailer. "Please help me lift him."

The jailer thrust his torch into a wall-bracket and bent to lift Robin, unaware that behind his back, the Friar had pulled a leather bottle from the folds of his cassock and was soaking the cuff of his long sleeve with its contents. Robin allowed himself to be helped to his feet, then he threw his arms around the jailer and held him with all his force. Before

the jailer could speak, a sleeve of rough
wet wool was clapped across his face and
held there by a hand with the grip of a
bear. The jailer's head filled with sweet
scents, and the last sound he heard was
his own heartbeat, galloping off like a
horse into the distance.

As the jailer sagged like a sack of flour,
Robin stared at the Friar in amazement.

"Is he dead?" he asked.

"He is asleep," replied the Friar. "I have given him a draught of henbane that will keep him in the deepest dreams until well after sunrise. Now we must pray that the key to your shackles is on the ring at his belt."

At the tables in the great hall, the Sheriff had drunk his fill. "I feel I would be failing in my duties as a host if I did not pay our prisoner a visit to make sure that he is comfortably lodged," he told Sir Guy. "Would you care to accompany me?"

"I'll wait for tomorrow and the sight of him swinging from the gallows," said Sir Guy, and when the Sheriff swaggered off towards the keep-tower, Sir Guy set out to stroll beneath the women's chambers in the hope of catching a glimpse of Marian. He was crossing the shadows of the stable-yard when a sleeve of rough wet wool was clapped across his face, and before he could claw it away his arms were caught and he was wrestled to the ground.

When the Sheriff reached the prison vaults, he was puzzled to find no sign of the jailer, but the door to Robin Hood's cell was locked and bolted, and when the Sheriff slid open the spyhole he heard the sound of gentle snoring in the darkness within.

"Sweet dreams, Robin Hood," the Sheriff said merrily.

He made his way out into the bailey and was surprised to see his men-at-arms running in all directions. He was even more surprised when the knight who was captain of the watch tried to tell him what was happening.

"We have not found him yet, my lord," he said, "but we have manned the walls. He cannot escape."

"What are you talking about?" asked the Sheriff.

"Surely you know the outlaw has

broken loose?" the knight asked him. "Sir Guy raised the alarm as he rode out."

"What is this nonsense?" thundered the Sheriff. "Are you telling me you opened the gates?"

"To Sir Guy of Gisburn, my lord," the knight explained. "He said he was riding out on your orders to raise the hue and cry in the town."

The Sheriff changed colour. "Fetch me a battering-ram!" he shouted. "The rest of you, search every corner. I want Robin Hood and I want him alive!"

They broke into the cell and found the jailer fast asleep, his ankles shackled to the wall. They woke and searched every guest in the hall, among them a friar who told them crossly that however fat he might look, he did not have an outlaw

hidden under his cassock. They even
searched every clothes-chest in the
women's chambers, but of Robin Hood
they found no trace.

At daybreak they found Sir Guy – fast
asleep in a sack in the rubbish pit behind
the kitchens – and the Sheriff knew then
that the man who had ridden out through
the castle gates on Sir Guy's horse and
wearing Sir Guy's surcoat had not been
Sir Guy of Gisburn at all.

The Sheriff climbed to the battlements and gazed down at the crowds teeming into Nottingham for the last day of the Fair. He watched his men searching the town house by house and knew as he watched that it was pointless. Robin must already be miles away. Even now, as the truth sank in and his rage began to boil, the Sheriff could not bring himself to admit that his perfect trap had failed, and that the bird had flown free.

4. Robin and Marian

When Sir Guy of Gisburn awoke and discovered the fool he had made of himself, facing Marian in his hour of shame was more than he could bear. He sent his squire to escort her wherever she wished to go, and Marian told the squire that she wished to go home. Sir Guy watched them setting out in the company of a jolly friar riding the fattest mule Sir Guy had ever seen.

They were riding north through Sherwood when a man with a red beard leapt out of the trees ahead of them and

notched an arrow to his bow. The squire
did not need to look twice to recognize
the champion archer of Nottingham Fair,
and he turned and galloped south as fast
as his horse would carry him, leaving
Marian and the Friar at the mercy of the
laughing outlaw and his companions,
who came swarming out of the trees to
greet them.

When Robin's eyes met Marian's, the laughter left him. "I owe you my life," he said. "How can I thank you?"

"You owe your life to the Friar," Marian told him, and she turned to her companion. "Will you tell me now how you knew my name and all that was in my heart for Robin?" she asked.

The Friar shook his head. "That is far too serious a matter to be discussed on an empty stomach," he said gravely.

"Then it's as well that Little John went hunting this morning," said Robin, and he led his guests to a hidden lodge deep in the forest where they feasted on venison and ale. Only when the Friar had eaten enough for two and drunk enough for three did he find the strength to tell Robin and Marian how he had witnessed their quarrel at daybreak.

"There was such beauty in the moment you met," he said. "It broke my heart when you quarrelled. I decided there and then that I would not rest until I had brought you together and made you man and wife."

"Will you marry us?" Marian asked eagerly.

"Will *you* marry *me*?" Robin asked Marian.

"With all my heart," she replied. "Yesterday I saw what it would be to live without you. I also saw how much you need a wife to keep you alive."

"Then I have won a prize greater than any golden arrow," said Robin, and he turned to the Friar. "I think we deserve to know the name of the man who is going to marry us."

The Friar blushed. "My friends call me Tuck," he said.

"Then Tuck we shall call you," said Robin. "Welcome to the brotherhood, Friar Tuck."

So it was that Robin and Marian stood beneath the arched boughs of the forest as Friar Tuck clasped their hands together and spoke words of blessing. They knew that for as long as Robin was

an outlaw, the truth of what they were to each other must never reach the Sheriff or Sir Guy. Their love would be lived whenever and wherever they were able to meet, and their meetings would always be far from towns and castles, deep in the secret heart of the greenwood.

MORE WALKER PAPERBACKS
For You to Enjoy

☐ 0-7445-2303-6   *Hannah and Darjeeling*
                      by Diana Hendry   £2.99

☐ 0-7445-2226-9   *Black Woolly Pony, White Chalk Horse*
                      by Jane Gardam   £3.99

☐ 0-7445-3177-2   *Tiger Roars, Eagle Soars*
                      by Ruskin Bond   £2.99

☐ 0-7445-3683-9   *Midnight Pirate, Midnight Party*
                      by Diana Hendry   £3.99

☐ 0-7445-5223-0   *Smart Girls*
                      by Robert Leeson   £3.99

☐ 0-7445-5203-6   *My Aunty Sal and the*
                      Mega-Sized Moose
                      by Martin Waddell   £3.50

☐ 0-7445-6025-X   *Seven Weird Days At Number 31*
                      by Judy Allen   £3.99

☐ 0-7445-6004-7   *Jeremy Brown of the Secret Service*
                      by Simon Cheshire   £3.99

☐ 0-7445-4302-9   *Creepe Hall*
                      by Alan Durant   £3.99